HOW TO DRIVE YOUR FAMILY CRAZY... ON VALENTINE'S DAY

Other Scholastic titles by Dean Marney:

How to Drive Your Family Crazy ... On Halloween

Pet-rified

HOW TO DRIVE YOUR FAMILY CRAZY on VALENTINE'S DAY

DEAN MARNEY

AN
APPLE
PAPERBACK

SCHOLASTIC INC.

New York Toronto London Auckland Sydney
Mexico City New Delhi Hong Kong

ISBN 0-439-15849-4

12 11 10 9 8 7 6 5 4 3 2 1   0/0 1 2 3 4 5/0

Printed in the U.S.A.   40

First Scholastic printing, January 1998
First printing, revised edition, January 2000

Originally titled:
The Valentine That Ate My Teacher

For my teachers

HOW TO DRIVE YOUR FAMILY CRAZY... on VALENTINE'S DAY

1

Hi, my name is Liz. I'm a little tired of being called Lizzie although I know everyone is still going to call me that. Being named Elizabeth is hard because people feel like they can call you anything. They call you Liz, Beth, Ellie, everything except George but mostly they call me Lizzie. I think I even like Elizabeth better than Lizzie; well, maybe not. It is just that Lizzie can be rhymed with too many things like dizzy Lizzie, Lizzie is having a tizzie, Lizzie is busy, frizzy Lizzie. You get my drift.

I don't like Valentine's Day and it's very soon, like in a couple of days. I *bought* my valentines this year. I'm really glad my mother didn't say I had to make them. She made me do them last year and mine were the dumbest in the class. I was embarrassed to sign my name. My mother can have some weird ideas.

She also said I had to make one for my brother whose name is Booger but you can call him Boog for short. His real name is Booker, but who cares? Anyway, I not only had to give him a valentine but I had to make it.

I used black paper and put a Halloween sticker on it. Well, that was part of the reason I got in trouble. I shouldn't have been in trouble at all, I was only trying to be imaginative. People are always saying, "You're creative, use your imagination," but when you do they bite your head off. You could barely see what I wrote to him on the valentine because the paper was black and I used a pencil, so I don't see what the big deal was. I wrote "Happy Valentine's Day you stupid nose-picking idiot." I was in trouble and couldn't watch TV for practically the rest of the year, well, actually a week. The fact was I didn't care because there was nothing on anyway.

My parents are strict beyond belief and it is starting to drive me crazy. They won't let me sleep over at anyone's house this year because they say it makes me too tired and every time I do it I'm sick for a week. I wanted to explain to them that staying up late was why you stay over at someone's house and I'd probably have gotten sick anyway but they wouldn't listen. They always have to be right.

"It's our job to ensure your health and safety," says my mom.

I think it is their job to ensure that I don't have any fun. I was being fined a quarter every time I said something that is critical of other people or myself. I was in the hole for three months of my allowance with no hope of ever catching up so they had to drop it.

If I said, "This dinner is disgusting," I got fined a quarter.

If I said, "Booger is an idiot," I got fined two quarters, one for the Booger and one for the idiot.

I shouldn't have been fined for saying that Booger is an idiot because I was only stating a true fact. They say they don't want me to grow up being a critical person but they are criticizing me for being critical. I'm not critical, I just tell the truth. Besides, I don't want to grow up to be a liar. Is it my fault that certain people do some obnoxious, stupid things?

For a perfect example, there's Sybil. She happens to be a new girl in my class who thinks she is something totally wonderful, but she's not. She's a hog and a half. She thinks everyone loves her and all she can talk about is herself and she doesn't go anywhere without these other girls that I call the fan club because they don't breathe until she tells them to.

Now is it critical to tell her to her face that she is a stupid stuck-up creep and she isn't the boss of the entire world? Or is it better to lie and let her run the entire school and decide who is cool and who isn't? Do you think she is getting a valentine from me? I don't think so.

That brings me to my main point, I hate Valentine's Day. I detest it for three reasons:

1. It's not a real holiday. If it was a real holiday we'd get a day off from school.

2. It is stupid. You eat too much candy and you feel sick.

3. Boys.

I also hate boys. My mom says you can't hate people. You can only prefer not to be around them or dislike their behavior. Forget that. I hate them for three reasons:

1. They're stupid.

2. They're mean.

3. They're really stupid.

When I say I hate boys that includes my stupid little brother but not my dad. He can be mean and stupid but he tries not to be. Everyone else doesn't have a clue.

--

2

This has been the worst winter of my life. It has lasted forever. It has been so long I can't remember what spring and summer are like. We've had a ton of snow this year, since before Thanksgiving, and now that it is February it is just starting to melt — a little.

The snow isn't pretty anymore. It isn't white. It's about two shades beyond a toxic-waste-looking color. You know, it's kind of gray with brown, black, yellow, and weird shades of sort of green. If you're totally stupid you need to be reminded you don't want to get near the yellow stuff. At this point you should probably just avoid all of it.

I caught Roberto eating some snow. I told him he was probably going to die and he should go to the school nurse and tell her to give him something to make him throw up or pump his stomach.

He told me, "Mind your own business. Don't be

telling me what to do. You are the bossiest dumb girl in the whole world."

Do you see how stupid boys are? I was trying to save his life. Did he care? Boys usually hate me.

The only girl all the boys like is Sybil, wouldn't you know. Stupid people are attracted to the dumb creep just like she is a magnet. There is this boy. I'm not even going to tell you his name because I can't stand him. He sits behind me on the bus and tells everyone he likes me. It is so gaggy.

Okay, to be honest, there is one boy I've kind of liked. His name is Scott and he gets in trouble in our class all the time. I can't figure him out though. Sometimes he acts like he likes me and then other times he totally ignores me.

I think it should always be spring by the first of February. But here it was February and it was still winter. Everything was so boring except we had a substitute teacher because ours had a nervous breakdown. She really didn't. I just like to say that because it sounds cool, like we were so bad we drove her crazy. It isn't lying if it is a joke.

She's on some kind of leave working in the district office to plan something and then train teachers to do something. Teachers are always doing that. She told us exactly what it was but I wasn't paying any attention. Anyway, she's coming back but meanwhile we have Mr. Bernstein.

Okay, I've only known him a couple of weeks, but I was thinking that maybe he also could be okay for a guy. My mother met him and then at the dinner table told everyone, "You would not believe how good-looking and charming Elizabeth's substitute teacher is. He's so handsome. I don't know how she's going to learn anything."

I could've died. So what if he's cute? Like I care?

Of course Booger started in with, "Lizzie loves her teacher. Lizzie loves her teacher."

"Can I beat him up?" I asked politely.

"Yes, of course Lizzie," my dad answered sarcastically, "like I'm going to let you resort to violence to settle your differences."

"Ignore your brother," said my mom. "It is the mature thing to do. Besides, he's only jealous."

"Of what?!" I screamed at the very tip-top of my lungs. I admit I sounded like a psycho woman. But my mother looked like a train had just come in through the front door and I'd invited it in.

"Psycho time," said my dad, trying to make a joke out of it but it made me even madder.

"Lizzie," snapped my mother, "stop overreacting. Perhaps you'd like to do the dishes by yourself."

"Yes," I screamed, "when I overreact it means I want to do the dishes!"

I got to do the dishes for a week and I couldn't watch TV. Sometimes I know how I get into things and get into trouble. Then sometimes I don't understand how it happens. I'm minding my own business and suddenly something happens and I'm in total trouble. I don't know why I started screaming. Sometimes I just do things that I don't think about. It's the story of my life.

In music class we sang this song called "Nobody Knows the Trouble I've Seen," and I almost started bawling because it was the story of my life. Except you could change it to nobody knows the weird stuff and trouble I've seen. I know weird backward and forward.

Sometimes late at night I lie in my bed and wonder, "Why me? Why does my life have to be like this? Why can't I be normal? Why can't I just be like everyone else? Why? Why? Why?"

You have to understand that things happen to me differently from other people. I'm totally serious. Strange and extraordinary things have happened to me. I'm talking *not* normal stuff. I never quite know exactly when they are going to happen and once they start, it seems I have absolutely no way of stopping them.

My only option is to ride them out like a sickening carnival ride. You want to throw up and you can't do anything until the ride is over. A hint that something is about to happen is that I run into this guy named Ralph. I am impressed that I even remembered his name.

You see, most of the time, I forget who he is and what his name is. I think he does it through some kind of hypnosis thing. My memories of him only come floating to the top of my brain sometimes or I'll dream about him or something. Then it is too late. I'm already in trouble.

When I get around Ralph, my life goes crazy. Some kids have an imaginary playmate. I have Ralph.

I found a note I wrote to myself last year and put in my sock drawer. It said, "Remember Ralph and what happened." I couldn't figure out what it meant so I threw the note away. It was later in the day that I remembered. That is why I started writing this stuff down. See how weird it is?

Since Christmas, nothing had been happening that was what you could classify as super-weird. There was little weird stuff but nothing that would make you think you'd lost your mind. Then I began seeing Ralph again.

I only saw his back, but I knew it was him. It seemed like everywhere I went he was there. He would be walking just ahead of me and then turn the corner and not be there. He'd be in a car speeding past. He would be sitting three rows up in the movie theater. He was everywhere. I thought I even saw him at the skating rink with his long black overcoat and a bright yellow scarf.

Every time I saw him I felt a little uneasy, like I could get sick but I wasn't really sick. This time,

I knew something was about to happen and I was waiting for the bomb to fall.

I was in class looking out the window and I saw Ralph again. He was walking across the playfield in the snow. He turned and waved at the school. I freaked because I knew he was waving at me.

"Liz," said Mr. Bernstein, "would you like to join the class?"

"Huh?" I said and the entire class laughed at me.

"Lizzie," said Mr. Bernstein, "try to concentrate."

I wrote a note to myself. "Have Mom call and find out why Mr. Bernstein hates me."

3

Later that same day I caught myself staring at Mr. Bernstein. I scared myself. It was totally insane and awful because I was wondering what his wife was like. Then I was pretending what it would be like if I were married to him. I can't believe how stupid and embarrassing it was.

Then he yelled at me for not paying attention again. I knew he hated me. I told my mom and of course she said, "That is ridiculous. Mr. Bernstein doesn't hate you. I'm sure he likes you."

"But he always yells at me," I offered as proof.

"Well, perhaps, you could stop the behavior that makes him yell at you," she said in a high-pitched voice that sounded like *she* didn't like me either.

"I don't do anything wrong," I mumbled. "He doesn't like me."

"Change your attitude, Elizabeth," she demanded.

"How do I do that?" I demanded back.

"By not being bratty right now," she said.

The next day Mr. Bernstein caught me running in the hall and yelled at me again. I tried to explain I was running away from Nancy who was going to slug me because I accidentally tripped her but he didn't care. He hates me. He wouldn't even listen. I'm going to flunk out.

In the classroom I slumped in the chair and got out my math book. I used to like math but I don't like it with Mr. Bernstein. He was standing over by Sybil's and Monica's desks and talking to them and laughing his fool head off. I couldn't believe that he liked them and not me.

After math we had science and we were studying the human circulatory system. There was this totally gross and disgusting picture of a human heart in our textbooks. I was sure I was going to vomit looking at it. Mr. Bernstein kept going on and on about it and asking us to identify the different parts of it. He made us find our pulse in our wrists and our necks.

I started feeling really weak and I couldn't lift my pencil. Then I looked down at the picture in the book. And all of a sudden it was as if the picture was a real-live beating heart, not a picture, and I could see it pumping right there on my desk. I shook my head and blinked several times and luckily it went back to being a picture.

Then we had to watch a video of a man having open-heart surgery. I couldn't believe it. The man, although he had the anesthesia mask on, looked like someone I'd seen before — me. And when they opened him up, instead of a human heart he had a black Halloween valentine made out of paper with stickers.

At that point, I saw tiny little stars and they weren't on the screen. They were dancing and jumping around right in front of my eyes. My ears started buzzing and I felt like I was falling backward into a tunnel.

I woke up. I'd fallen off my chair. Mr. Bernstein was above me and I could smell his spicy cologne. He was smiling at me and telling everyone to get back.

"You fainted," he said. "Lie still. We'll want to get you checked out before we move you. You're going to be fine."

I could've died of the embarrassment. I hate everyone looking at me. I had to lie on the floor until the nurse came and checked me out. Then the nurse and Mr. Bernstein took me to the office and they called my mom to come get me.

My mother came and stared at me like I'd done something bad. "What did you do?" she whispered.

"I don't know," I said, and I wanted to cry but I held it back.

"We think she fainted," said the nurse. "They were studying the heart."

"And . . ." my mother said.

"I think she got uncomfortable and fainted. It happens to some people. However, you should probably call her physician."

We got in the car while a bunch of kids stared at me some more through the school windows. My mother started acting a lot nicer.

"Your uncle passes out every time he has to give blood," she said.

"I don't know what happened," I sighed. "It made me feel weird."

At home, my mother called the doctor and he said it was probably nothing but to watch me. Like they don't watch every move I make as it is now. Right before I went to bed, Mr. Bernstein called to make sure I was okay.

"She's fine," said my mom. "Do you want to talk to her?"

I could have killed her.

"Hello?" I said.

4

"**H**i Lizzie," said Mr. Bernstein. "Are you okay?"

"I'm fine, really," I said.

"Got a little queasy, huh?" he asked. "Has this happened before?"

"No," I said.

"Well, I'll be more careful next time," he said. "That video can be rather gruesome. I assume you kids have seen so much gory stuff on movies and TV that I didn't worry about it."

"I didn't think it was bad," I lied to him. "Sometimes weird things happen to me."

"Okay . . ." laughed Mr. Bernstein. "You take care and I'll see you tomorrow. We'll do something else in science. Any suggestions?"

"Oh, oh, I don't know," I said, sounding so dumb I cannot believe it. Why couldn't I think of something intelligent to say? Why couldn't I have said, "Physics or chemistry or E equals mc squared?"

"See you tomorrow then," said Mr. Bernstein.

Then I did the most stupid thing I've ever heard of. "Have fun," I said, like a complete idiotic doof. What was happening to me?

"Huh?" he said.

"I mean good-bye," I said.

I got off the phone and screamed at my mother, "I'm such an idiot. Why did you let him talk to me?! He's really going to hate me now and he'll think I'm a total geek! Why do you do these things to me?"

My mother didn't even look shocked. Maybe because I was already grounded.

"Go lie down, Lizzie," is all she said.

I went up to my room and thought about my conversation. I thought, *What do you care what he thinks about you?* I thought back, *I don't, I'm being ridiculous.*

Then I couldn't stop thinking of ways I could prove to him I wasn't a complete moron. I wanted him to know that my fainting during the heart show was just a weird coincidence. The guy in the movie looked like me and my book was going crazy. Nothing makes me queasy. At least nothing used to.

We used to have this book that showed what first, second, and third degree burns looked like. I was the only kid in the neighborhood that could look at it or even touch the picture. I also want to throw up when Booger picks his nose but I don't. I've fallen off my bike a million times and I've practically bled to death and never passed out. Some freak weird thing was happening to me and to prove it, something else weird happened. I saw the funny guy Ralph fly by my upstairs window.

"Help?" I squeaked because my voice had suddenly gone someplace else in my body.

There he was again. He was waving at me outside my window like some vampire ready to break in and turn me into some horrible monster that always wears black dresses.

"Go away," I quietly screeched.

I tried to move but I couldn't. I was frozen with fright. Ralph was still floating by my second-story window and he was holding up a sign in the shape of a heart. The print was too tiny. I could barely read it and I wasn't going to get any closer to the window than I already was. I made out a couple of words. One was "crack" and the other was "jealousy."

Then he was gone. He vanished into thin air, well almost. He was gone and I heard this thud so I looked out my window. He had fallen to the ground, hitting the snow hard enough to make a crater. But he got up, brushed himself off, smiled, and waved up at me. He then turned and walked down the street. I could finally talk.

"Mom!" I yelled down the stairway. "There was a vampire holding a valentine sign outside my window! I think his name is Ralph."

"Lie down," she yelled back. "You're dreaming.

Do you have to be so dramatic about every-thing?"

I got out this medical book we have that ex-plains all about the body and I looked at all the pictures of the heart. They stayed pictures. Noth-ing happened except I started thinking these bizarre thoughts about love.

"Why do people think love comes from our hearts?" I asked the book.

I guess it was a good thing it didn't answer.

5

Get this — keeling over in class made me popular throughout the entire school until about lunchtime. Then it wore off. I didn't seem to have what it takes to stay popular for long periods of time.

I asked Sybil why she hadn't invited me to her birthday party. She said, "You don't get it. You just don't get it."

I get it. I knew she was talking about popularity. I was really angry.

I don't want you to think I'm totally obsessed about being popular. I don't care except sometimes I think it might be fun to be super-popular so you wouldn't have to worry about it. The fact is I suppose you still have to worry about staying popular. I hear Sybil's party was the worst anyway.

I'm not in the nerd group or the popular group. I'm in the middle. I have tons of friends, really. Sybil and her fan club just aren't among them.

Anyway, stupid me raised my hand and asked Mr. Bernstein, "Why do people think we love from our hearts?"

The entire class groaned. They wished I'd passed out again.

"Good question, Lizzie," he said.

I looked over toward Sybil to make sure she'd heard him. She wasn't paying any attention and I noticed she wasn't getting yelled at.

"Great question, Lizzie, and I happen to know the answer. It is really quite simple. The heart has always been considered the center of the body. Love has always been considered the center of our lives. My understanding is that we matched up the two."

"Oh," I said, like I was really thinking hard about what he said. I thought he'd be impressed and at least hang around my desk sometime. However, Sybil just had to raise her ugly little hand and ask her own question.

"Speaking of love, who started Valentine's Day?" she asked.

He said, "Oh, uh," about three times like he'd really been stumped. "I don't know," he laughed at Sybil. "But guess what? I love not knowing because that means I get to learn something new."

Then he tossed me out of the room. I'm just kidding. He sent me to the library to look it up. I practically dislocated my shoulder trying to volunteer to go find out for the class. I sneered at Sybil when he picked me.

Lucky for me, I'm good at looking things up. I love the library. Unlucky for me, he sent me out right before science. It was my big chance to see if something would happen and I would faint again. Everyone was going to be watching me. They had been waiting all day for this moment and I was going to let them down.

Another unlucky thing was that I thought I saw Ralph's back going into the janitor's closet. I hurried past, dying to open the door and scared to death to do it. Right when I was in front of the door, someone tripped me.

Oh no, I thought. *I'm being abducted.* Wrong! It was only Scott.

"Why'd you do that?" I asked.

"I don't know," he said.

Boys don't know anything. It is totally ridiculous. "What are you doing out here?" I demanded.

"I have to take the attendance down to the office," he answered.

"I'm going to the library," I reminded him.

"Oh, ya," said Scott. "I knew that."

"Well, bye," I said.

Scott used to like me, which is maybe why I kind of like him but I'm not sure he does now. He did trip me. I don't understand completely but when boys like you they do intentionally mean things. It kind of confuses me. Why would you be

21

mean to someone you like or you want to like you? I'm not going to think about it. I have the feeling I'm not going to understand it or change it.

I went to the library and Mr. Brown was there and he was kind of mad I was there because he was doing something else but he helped me anyway. We searched the encyclopedia and the computer and found a book that was just about Valentine's Day. I sat at a table and started looking at it.

"Weird," I said quietly.

Get this. Valentine's Day started as a Roman holiday a zillion years ago. It was on February 15. However, it wasn't called Valentine's Day then.

Initially it was a holiday to celebrate the Roman god, Lupercus, who was in charge of sheep and shepherds. It was the holiday to do stuff for him and ask him to keep the sheep safe and especially to keep the wolves away. Well, it was getting so there weren't that many wolves around so they didn't need the holiday anymore. It changed into being a holiday for Juno, who was queen of the Roman gods.

She was the goddess in charge of marriage, which is kind of lame. If I were queen of all the Roman gods I would have put myself in charge of hitting people with lightning, or man-eating lions or something cool. But, she must have wanted to be queen of marriage. One thing they did on her holiday was all the young women would write their names on pieces of paper and put them in a jar. Then the young men would pull a name out and then they were a couple for the holiday. They probably put on clean togas and went to the coliseum together. There they ate Roman snacks and watched the lions eat some people. If the young woman didn't like the boy, she pushed him into the ring to get eaten — just kidding.

Then the Romans became Catholic and the Pope, Pope Gelasius, really hated Juno's holiday because it was pagan. He tried to stop the holiday but people thought it was too much fun. Maybe the jar thing was more fun than it sounded.

So he tried to stop it another way. He said that they could have a holiday but it was going to be about something else. He thought up a saint he could honor and he came up with one called Saint Valentine. He picked him because he died on February 14, which is pretty close to Juno's holiday on the fifteenth.

A bizarre thing is that Pope Gelasius probably knew which Valentine he was honoring but there were several Saint Valentines. People aren't sure now which one he meant, maybe all of them. Most of the people who study church history think it was probably one of two Saint Valentines. Those two Valentines, besides having the same name, were both priests and both had their heads cut off by Emperor Claudius, who was called "Claudius the Cruel." I think his name sounds like a professional wrestler.

Claudius made this ruling that no one could get married. His reasoning was that people didn't want to go to war after they got married. They missed their wives and families too much to leave them.

One Saint Valentine married people in secret anyway. It wasn't exactly a good secret. Claudius found out and put him in jail. Then he beheaded him.

The other Saint Valentine was in jail for being a Christian. While he was in there, he performed a miracle on the jailer's blind daughter so she could see. The same Claudius didn't want this to happen. He was such a bad guy and a jerk he had this Saint Valentine killed, too. Maybe Claudius had a thing against the name.

Pope Gelasius planned his new Saint Valentine's Day to be a religious celebration but it didn't work out that way. People probably wanted to do something besides go to church. They still liked Juno's holiday because it was about love and junk and was fun. Over a long time, the people sort of won. Even though we kept the name of Valentine, the day started being less and less about the Saint Valentine and more and more about love and marriage.

"Does the school board know about this?" I asked Mr. Brown.

6

I left the library and headed back to class. On the way, three things happened. All three things were weird but two of them were very weird.

First, I saw this girl who was younger than myself. She was in the hall because she was in trouble. She was upset and you could tell she was trying not to cry. I had this incredible urge to go up and hug her. I didn't because she probably would've slugged me. Then I could have spent my entire life in the hall with her. I felt really sad for her though. That's when something very peculiar happened.

The girl started vibrating like something was shaking her. Every part of her was moving and then she froze. However, she wasn't the little girl anymore, she was a little girl that looked like me.

She had my face. She was my double but younger. We even had the same clothes on. I felt dizzy and confused. I shook my head hard enough to give myself a headache and then I looked at her again. This time she didn't look like me at all.

She was staring at me like I was crazy so I had to say something. "I'm in trouble all the time. Don't worry about it. It doesn't mean anything." She almost smiled.

The second thing that happened was I saw Scott again. What is with him? I wondered if he were stalking me or something.

"Hi," he said. "Going back to class?"

"Ya," I replied as cool as I could make it sound.

"Oh," he said.

We didn't talk for a minute.

"I'm going back, too," he said.

"I kind of figured that," I whispered because we were walking past a classroom with the doors open.

"Oh, I almost forgot," said Scott, reaching into his pocket. "A guy in the hall — he must be a new teacher — gave this to me and told me to give it to you."

It was a business card. On one side was printed "Ralph." That's it, just Ralph. I flipped the card over. There was a handwritten note and it said, "Go to the basement. I have an important message."

We were almost back at our classroom when the third weird thing happened. Over the loudspeaker came this huge booming voice. The volume was up so high that I swear you could see

26

and feel the sound waves moving down the hall.

"Elizabeth, please come to the basement as soon as possible!"

"What did I do now? Where's the basement?" I asked Scott.

"Are you nuts? There is no basement to this building."

"Well you heard the announcement. I'm supposed to go to the basement," I told him.

"What announcement?" questioned Scott, looking very confused.

"The announcement just now." I kind of laughed so he wouldn't feel so stupid.

"Just now?" he demanded.

"Ya," I said.

"I didn't hear an announcement," he said.

"Oh yeah," I said laughing, "it was so quiet you couldn't hear it?"

"You're nuts," he said flatly. "There hasn't been an announcement."

"There has, too," I said. "Knock it off."

"Check at the office if you don't believe me."

"I have to get back to class," I said, knowing that if I went to the office I would be in trouble.

"You're lying and you can't admit it," insisted Scott.

"I am not," I pouted. "You're the one that is lying."

"Then prove it." He stood looking at me.

I was really mad then. Nobody calls me a liar

and gets away with it. I'd go to the stupid office. We turned the corner and went down another hall toward the office. I marched up to the secretary's counter.

"Was there a message on the loudspeaker for me?" I asked.

"There was no message on the loudspeaker for you," said the secretary very slowly.

"See," sneered Scott.

"Are you sure?" I asked again.

"What are you doing back here?" the secretary asked Scott.

"Nothing," said Scott.

"Return to your class both of you," snapped the secretary, who had a bad attitude if you ask me. She didn't need to get all bent out of shape just because someone asked her a question. That is just my opinion.

I asked the secretary who now totally hated me, "Do we have a basement to this building?"

"Get back to class," she repeated. "This is a one-story building. There is no basement."

"Oh," I said, trying to make a joke out of it by laughing a little, "just kidding."

7

As we walked back to class, I must have looked like I was going to faint again because Scott kept asking, "Are you okay?"

I didn't want to say, "No, I'm hearing things that other people don't hear. I'm not okay," so I said nothing.

We walked into class together and that total twit Sybil goes, "Isn't that cute? They were together."

Her fan club laughed like she was the world's funniest comedian. Words cannot begin to describe how much I disliked them at that moment. Why was Sybil trying to humiliate me? I couldn't take it anymore. I know I may sound psycho but she was really getting to me.

I was at the point that if she even looked at me I was going to . . . well, I wasn't going to be responsible for my actions. I wished that Sybil would get an instant attack of the worst acne the world had ever seen. I wanted warts to cover her entire body. I wished her scalp would be all scabby and everyone would think she was disgusting.

"That is enough, class," said Mr. Bernstein. "Scott and Lizzie, please take your seats."

I sat down, still furious. Then for a second it was like I wasn't there. I mean I must have been there but something happened to me. It was for only an instant and I blinked my eyes and it stopped. In the meantime, everything had changed.

Now don't ask me how things were different because I don't know exactly. Things just felt different. It felt like the air had changed or something. It felt heavier. The lights' hum was heavier. My arms felt heavy. Everything felt heavy.

The class had finished science and was moving on to spelling. I waited for Mr. Bernstein to ask me what I found out about Valentine's Day but he never said a word. I slowly raised my heavy hand.

"Yes, Lizzie?" he almost glared at me, or I thought he did.

"Don't you want to know what I found out about Valentine's Day?" I gasped. I was having trouble breathing the heavy air.

"Later," he said really fast and forceful like he didn't care at all.

My feelings were hurt. I felt like a sword had fallen on my head. He was acting so strangely. He *must* have felt it. His forehead was sweating. He looked like he was getting sick. Then I saw something distinctly different.

A red paper cupid on the wall was pointing to it. In the far corner of the room there was a huge crack running from the floor to the ceiling. I'd never seen that crack before in my life. It was like the Grand Canyon on our wall. You could've driven a bus through it. Well, you could have at least put your whole arm in it. It was like the two walls were being pulled apart.

I raised my hand because I thought maybe the place was starting to cave in like the neighbor's carport did because it had too much snow on the roof. I also thought that maybe we'd had an earthquake and I missed it.

"Mr. Bernstein," I interrupted, still having trouble breathing, "I happened to notice the crack in the corner and I was just wondering if . . ."

He cut me off and yelled, "Be quiet, Lizzie! I'm trying to teach!"

"I'm only concerned about safety," I defended myself.

"Well maybe you'd feel safer in the hall!" he yelled again.

"No, sir," I said. "I'll be quiet."

I sat there watching that crack and it was getting even larger. It looked like it was starting to spread across the edge of the ceiling toward the light fixtures. There was also something coming out of it. It was green, slimy, oozing smoke that moved like it was alive.

I tapped Alex, the boy in front of me, hard. "What is that stuff coming out of the crack in the corner?" I whispered super-fast.

"Shut up," said Alex, "and quit poking me."

"Elizabeth," yelled Mr. Bernstein. "What is wrong now?"

"It is just that the crack in the corner . . ."

"Go to the hall," he demanded in a deeper voice than I'd ever heard.

"What?" I asked.

"You heard me," he growled.

"But," I said weakly, "it's getting larger and stuff is coming out of it and I was just asking if it was safe."

"That's enough!" he shouted. "Go to the hall now!"

I was in shock. I'd never seen Mr. Bernstein be mean to anyone. I got out of my seat and walked to the door.

Scott's desk is by the door. When I dragged myself past him he whispered, "What are you doing?"

"What Mr. Bernstein told me to do," I huffed.

Scott looked at me like I was nuts. "He did not," he said. "You had better sit down or you're going to get into trouble."

"I have to do what he says," I whispered back. "He's the teacher."

"You're nuts," said Scott.

"Whatever," I said.

Mr. Bernstein was ignoring me and writing something on the board. He was writing but where he wrote it looked blank. The green stuff was all around him curling around his body all the way to his neck.

The last thing I saw as I walked out the door was Sybil laughing hysterically at me. I glared at her before I left.

8

I had just gotten out into the hall when the fire alarm went off. I thought, *Oh, great, it's a fire drill.* Then again, no one was acting like it was a fire drill. No one came out of their classrooms. What was I supposed to do? I scratched my head and pulled something out of my hair. It was a scab. I almost hurled.

The fire alarm was still blaring and I wondered if it could be a real fire. If I stayed where I was, would I be burned alive or overcome from smoke inhalation? For some insane reason what popped into my head was this story that my teacher in second grade read to us.

It was about this girl who hated taking piano lessons and was mad all the time because her parents made her practice every day after school. Her parents kept telling her that one day she'd thank them for making her play the piano. Well, one day there was a fire at school and everyone was going crazy and no one would stay in line to file out safely. There just happened to be a piano in the hallway and a teacher yelled, "Does anyone play the piano?"

"I do," volunteered the girl and they hustled her to that piano. She had memorized all these marches so she was ready to go. She played her little fingers off and all the children lined up in single file, marched out of that school, and no one was burned beyond recognition. She bravely kept playing until the last child left the school, and then a firefighter carried her out because she had collapsed. Outside, in front of the whole school, they declared her a hero. She went home and thanked her parents for making her practice.

I was trying to picture myself playing a piano during a fire and I thought I looked pretty stupid seeing as how I didn't know how to play the piano. I play the cello. However, if I did know how to play, I would have played a rock song and gotten people out of there fast.

Suddenly the alarm stopped and the loudspeaker squelched and a man's voice whispered, "Go to the basement, Lizzie."

I looked around. What was I supposed to do? I knew I was probably hearing things. It was too bizarre and why was the man whispering? Did he think he wouldn't be heard on a loudspeaker system? I could hear my heart beating really loud and it felt like it was located in my ears and not in my chest. Then over the sound of my heart I heard someone crying their eyes out, wailing down the hall.

"You're not nuts," I repeated to myself over and over, "and there is no basement."

I peeked through the window in the door to my classroom. Everyone was acting like nothing was going on. The green ooze stuff had completely taken over the classroom and they didn't seem to care. It covered everything and everyone from the floor to the ceiling.

The loudspeaker squelched again. "There is always a basement," the man's voice said.

"Okay," I screamed and then put my hand over my mouth. I knew I was going to be in big trouble for raising my voice in the hallway especially while classes were going on.

However, nothing happened. No one came out to see what I was doing.

"Okay," I said, "this is too weird. What is going on?"

I waited a little longer but still nothing was happening. I was trying to ignore my thumping heartbeat. I decided to go back into the classroom. I imagined the worst thing that could happen would be that I would get yelled at and thrown out into the hall again. I peered into the window one more time and everyone was still there looking green, almost as if they were underwater or aliens from another planet.

I put my hand on the latch to my room and pushed down. It was locked.

"They locked me out," I said under my breath. "It was probably Sybil, that little creep."

I knocked lightly on the door. No one heard me. It was like I didn't exist. I knocked louder. They still ignored me. Finally, I kicked and beat on the door with both my fists.

There was no response and I got freaky scared. I knew something was very, very wrong. I tried to think of the best thing to do. I thought and I did what any smart person would do in the situation. I went running down the hall hysterically screaming.

I didn't know what I'd do when I got there, but I did know I was heading toward the office. I turned the corner but it wasn't there. I thought I must've been confused and taken a wrong turn. Instead of the office there was a door marked "Basement." I was shaking with fright.

Okay, it is time to tell you that I have a long history of dealing with basements. I'm gradually getting over my fear of my own basement at home. I still don't go down there to hang out in the dark for something to do. But I also don't get sick at the thought of going down there anymore.

However, this was different. And I wasn't about to go through a door marked "Basement" in my school when I knew it didn't have a basement.

At least I didn't think I was going to go through it.

I went down another hall and ended up back in the same place. I have no idea how I did it but there I was in front of this door marked "Basement" again.

"Mom! Dad!" I yelled. "Help!"

While I was standing there yelling, a note was slipped under the door toward me. I stopped yelling and picked it up.

It said, "There is enough love for everyone."

"Someone is messing with my head," I said, and I was getting more mad than afraid. I grabbed the handle of the door and opened it up. I must have looked quite surprised as I fell into the principal's office.

9

So, how do you explain why you're in the principal's office when you don't have a clue about what is going on?

"Can I help you?" said the principal. "Usually we knock before we open a door and barge in."

"Sorry . . . well," I said, standing there fidgeting and wondering what to do.

"Lizzie, what is going on? Did you get sent from class? Are you in trouble? Do you have a hall pass? Are you ill?"

"No," I blurted out. "I thought I heard that I was supposed to report to the basement but there isn't a basement and then I heard the fire alarm so I couldn't figure out what was happening. I couldn't think of where to go because my classroom door was locked so I came here but I thought this was the basement and then I opened the door and it was your office and . . ."

"Wait, please," she said. "That's enough. I do not want to know any more. I think it would be best that you return to your class. You're with Mr. Bernstein aren't you?"

I nodded.

She continued, "I'll deal with him and then I'll call your mother. I hope you're not trying to pull something."

I went back to my classroom. There was no green ooze. There wasn't even a crack for it to come out of. I sat down, confused, dazed, and a little embarrassed. I ran my fingers through my hair. I didn't have any scabs.

"What happened to you?" said Lisa, who sits next to me.

Mr. Bernstein noticed me. "Glad you could make it back," he said. "Where have you been?"

"Been?" I whispered.

"We'll solve it later," he said.

Lisa whispered, "You left to go to the bathroom but you must have gone somewhere else because I went looking for you and you weren't there."

"What do you mean?" I asked her.

"Mr. Bernstein told me to go look for you."

"He's the one that sent me out in the hall," I said.

"Huh?" said Lisa. "You asked to go to the restroom."

"I did?"

"You did."

Then Lisa acted very excited. "You must have passed out again."

I barely heard her. I was too busy noticing that Mr. Bernstein was again standing over at Sybil's desk laughing and talking and acting like they were best friends. I couldn't hear what they were saying but Sybil thought it was extremely funny. She was laughing and I could see clear across the room that funny way her nostrils flare in and out like fish gills when she laughs.

Then the day was over and I was on the bus on the way home. It had been a horrible day. I was so confused. I didn't know what was real and what I was imagining.

I was sitting on the bus minding my own business with my best friend, Bob. Don't get any ideas because she's a girl. She just has a weird name.

Anyway she was picking at her fingernails trying to scrape off this ugly kind of green and brown polish she'd put on. It was starting to irritate me.

"It's called camouflage," she told me. "It was on sale."

"I can believe that," I said.

She was talking my ear off about her family and some dumb stuff that happened to her at school that she had already told me. She wanted to tell me for the nine hundredth time about some dumb thing that happened at the skating rink. This boy, Richard, wanted to hold her hand. I could've cared less.

I wanted to scream because I needed to talk about *me*. All this weird stuff was happening and no one cared. I tried to interrupt her about sixty thousand times but she went right on.

I finally just accepted it and zoned out while she told me about her boring piano lessons. I was beginning to wonder why we were best friends. I looked around the bus for anyone else I could talk to. I saw Scott.

Scott doesn't normally ride my bus. I wondered what he was doing there. Then I realized who he was sitting by . . . Sybil with her flabby nostrils just flapping to beat the band.

"Look at that." I chiseled my way into Bob's conversation. "Scott is sitting by Sybil and he doesn't even belong on this bus. I feel like telling on them and getting them both thrown off."

"They're not doing anything," said Bob.

I couldn't believe she would be on their side.

"How can you say that?"

"Did you know Sybil and I have the same piano teacher? She's better than I am," Bob began again, and she told me about what Sybil played at some dumb stupid recital like I ever cared.

"Has she ever played for a fire?!" I yelled at Bob. "Well, has she?!"

Then that insane boy behind me started staring at me again. I could feel his beady little eyes on the back of my head. I whipped around and said, "Stop looking at me."

All he could lamely say was, "Hi, Lizzie."

My bus stop came and I shoved my way to the door.

"Watch it, Elizabeth," said the bus driver. "No one likes pushy people."

"Get out of my way," I yelled at Booger when we were out of hearing distance of the bus driver.

Pushing him aside into a snowbank, I stormed down the sidewalk toward my house. I would have liked to storm all the way home, it felt good. However, I fell because I wasn't watching where I was going. I hit some ice and went flying. I sailed through the air and could've landed on my bottom but oh, no, I had to go headfirst into a snow and mud pile.

To make it worse, Sybil came running up behind me to save me.

"Are you okay?" she asked, pretending like she cared.

"I'm fine," I moaned, getting up.

"Oops," she said, pointing to where I had landed.

The snow was distinctly yellow.

10

"Lizzie!" my mother yelled the minute I hit the doorway.

I didn't want to answer her. "What?" I said as pleasantly as possible.

"What were you doing wandering in the halls at school? And what are you doing telling the principal that you're hearing voices telling you to go to the basement? She thinks you need a hearing test. I'm not sure you don't need a psychiatric evaluation."

"What's that?" I asked.

"Don't get me started," she said, but she was already started. I mean *really* started.

"I told her there was nothing wrong with your hearing. There is much wrong with your judgment, however," she went on. She was a lot madder than I'd seen her for at least a week.

"Why are you home? Did you get off work early?" I tried to change the subject.

"I got called at work by your principal and I

needed to come home," she said, glaring at me.

"Oh," I said, at first feeling guilty but then being angry with everyone for not believing me.

"Why is everyone mad at me? It isn't like I've done anything wrong and everyone is yelling at me. I fell down on the ice into some yellow snow and I'm hurt." I tried to limp a little while walking around the room. "See?"

"Do I need to remind you what happens to people who hear voices? Does Joan of Arc ring a bell?"

"Yes," I said.

"And what, pray tell, happened to her?" she asked.

"I don't know." But I did. "You don't have to be sarcastic."

"She was burned at the stake," my mother said.

"Well I'm not Joan of Arc!" I screamed and I dragged myself with a huge limp over to the stairway.

"Young lady," said my mother, "get back here. I'm not through with you."

"I have a headache," I tried, "and I'm feeling nauseated. I know I'm going to throw up."

She completely ignored my pain and said, "Write an apology to the principal. I'll sign it. Make sure that you include the phrase, 'I'll never do it again.' Now hurry up and come down and unload the dishwasher."

"Make Booger, I mean Booker," I said. "I did it yesterday."

"He's doing his homework," said my mom.

"Maybe I have homework. Did you think of that?"

"Do it," she said.

"He never does anything wrong. You always make me do stuff and he never has to."

"That is not true," she said.

I stood there looking at her. I wasn't going to move.

"Fine," she said. "How grounded do you want to be?"

I turned and mumbled under my breath as I started hobbling up the stairs, "Till I'm eighty-five."

They didn't talk about it at dinner. I guess it was over. I wrote the stupid note and my mom signed it. I knew my dad wanted to lecture me, too, but he didn't. My mom must have told him it wouldn't do any good. She does that.

Besides, they couldn't notice me. Booger was once again telling them the smallest details of his stupid life and they were fascinated by every breath he took. So what if he won the spelling bee.

"Good for you," my mom kept saying.

"Great," said my dad.

I'd try to enter the conversation by correcting some of the dumber stuff Booger was saying that wasn't at all true and they just jumped down my throat.

"Lizzie," said my mom quietly, "we're listening to Booker and he's doing fine without your added negative comments."

"I'm just trying to be part of the conversation," I said.

"Can you find a positive way to do that?" my dad asked.

"No," I answered. At least I was honest and what does honesty get you? It means you get to do the dishes for the rest of your miserable life.

I turned on the radio while I was slaving away. A song was playing and I didn't like it but my hands were wet so I couldn't change it. Finally it was over and then the DJ said, "And this next song is for Lizzie."

I figured it was another Lizzie but I wanted to listen anyway. There was a pause.

"Well, what is it?" I demanded.

The DJ played a song called "Jealousy."

"Obviously, not for me," I said, and switched off the radio, wet hands or not.

11

I wrote a note to myself: "If something seems unreal it probably is." The phone was ringing and then my dad said it was for me.

"Hello?" I said.

"Hi, Lizzie," said a boy's voice.

"Who is this?" I asked.

"Guess," answered the voice.

"Ya, right," I said, "who is this?"

"Guess," said the voice again.

"I know who it is," was my guess.

There was a long pause.

"How did you know?"

"Really?" I said, amazed. "Like I see you every day sitting behind me on the bus and staring at me."

"Well . . ." said the boy, and don't ask because I'm not telling you his name.

There was another long pause. Talking to boys is so much fun. They never know what to say.

All of a sudden out of the blue he spits out, "I know Scott likes you. Do you like him?"

"What?" I said.

"You heard me," he said.

My mother interrupted by yelling from the living room, "Elizabeth, who is it, darling?"

"It's for me, Mom."

"Don't be on the phone too long. I'm expecting a call."

"I'd better go," I said to him.

"Do you like him?" he pressed.

"I don't know," I said.

"Come on," he pleaded, "tell me."

"I've got to go," I said. "Bye."

"Oh, okay, well, bye, I guess," he said.

I hung up the phone and my mother interrogated me.

"Who was that?"

"Just a boy on my bus."

"What did he want?" she asked, smiling like she was really interested.

"Nothing," I said, and I had this horrible urge to tell a lie. I did everything to stop myself but I could feel it forming in me like a tapeworm. It was working its way up through my body until I had to cough it out.

"He wanted to know what our math assignment was."

"Did you tell him?" asked my mom.

49

"Uh-huh," I nodded.

My brother was practicing the piano, loudly.

"Does he have to do that?" I asked, changing the subject.

"You have to practice to be good at things," said my mother.

I thought it was stupid. So what if everyone was better than I was. Why bother?

"Mom?" I asked. "What is love anyway?"

"What?" she answered.

"Nothing," I said. "Just kidding."

12

I lay in bed and thought about love. That didn't take very long. I wondered if I'd ever be really in love with a boy.

Then I thought about what a creep Sybil is and how it isn't fair that everyone likes her. I didn't know why they didn't like me the way they do her. What is so cool about Sybil? Why was Scott even hanging around her? Then I got worried that maybe Bob would start to like Sybil.

I got out of bed and wrote myself another note. "If Bob likes Sybil, she is no longer my friend."

Back in bed, I had a dream. I dreamed I pushed Sybil off a cliff but somehow we switched places and I was the one that was falling. I woke up before I hit the ground. I remember looking up as I was falling toward the ground and watching Sybil standing there staring at me with this hurt look.

I woke up thinking, She is such a big creep. I went downstairs for breakfast and my dad and Booger had made oatmeal.

"It's good for you," my dad said, giving me a huge scoop.

"Where's the sugar?" I sneered.

"Oops," said my dad, laughing. "I was hoping you wouldn't notice."

"What?" I asked.

"We're out of sugar," said my dad.

"How could we be out of sugar?" I questioned.

"We don't know," said Booger and my dad together like it was an inside joke.

"You know what we have instead of sugar?" quizzed my dad, being funny.

"I don't want to know. Really, I don't want to know," I said. My dad can be slightly weird and kind of irritating.

"Ta-da," he said as he whipped a bowl out from behind his back. The bowl was full of those little sugary candy hearts with little sayings on them. "They'll be terrific on your oatmeal, sort of a valentine oatmeal experience."

"Uh-huh," said Booger with his mouth full. He thought it was great.

"You've got to be kidding."

They weren't. They were both eating their oatmeal like it was the best thing they had ever had.

"I can't believe you're eating candy for breakfast," I said — like I had never done it and I was the parent.

"Lighten up, Lizzie. It isn't like we eat this way

every day," said my dad. He's right. He's usually the one telling us to improve our diets.

"Where's Mom?" I asked.

"Already at work," said my dad. "She had a breakfast meeting."

"Okay," I said, and I put some hearts on the mush. I like those little hearts but I wasn't going to let them think I liked their idea. I tasted it.

It was pretty good. I mean those things are made of sugar and dye. I like both of those things.

"Good, huh?" prompted my dad.

"Yes," I said and added, "but Mom would think it was dumb."

Booger said to me, "So what," and then to whoever was listening which was no one, "My heart says I'm terrific."

I looked down at one of my hearts and it said, "Love is always present." I had to look superclose because the print was so tiny to fit all the words on the heart but that is what it said.

Booger said, "This one says 'You're cute.' "

I looked at the rest of mine. They all said, "Love is always present." I mean I looked at more than ten of them. I looked through the ones in the sugar bowl and they all said the same thing.

I thought, Isn't it just like Booger to pick out all the best hearts and leave me the "Love is always present"?

"Hurry up," said my dad. "We have to get to school."

I noticed a plastic sack full of hearts on the counter and grabbed a handful of the hearts and put them in my pocket. I rinsed off my bowl and stuck it in the dishwasher. Of course Booger left the milk out and I had to put it away.

We missed the bus so we caught a ride with my dad. Booger got to sit in the front seat and my dad let him choose the radio station. He picked the country station just to make me crazy.

"Do we have to listen to this?" I said.

We arrived at school and I saw Bob outside.

"Do you like Sybil?" I asked.

"I don't even know her," said Bob. "She doesn't even say hi to me."

"But would you be her friend?" I grilled.

"I don't know," said Bob. "Why?"

"I'm just checking," I said.

We went into our classroom and I immediately inspected the corner. There were no visible big cracks. I went over and examined it closely. There were some small cracks but they'd probably been there forever. I guessed I was the only thing that was cracked.

I wondered if maybe I hit my head sometime and it did permanent damage, like the time I went in-line skating and ran into the side of that truck. It wasn't moving but I was and then I wasn't. I probably had a concussion and no one bothered to find out or tell me that I would think there were cracks in the walls that weren't really there.

Sybil was telling Mr. Bernstein some story about her dog. We don't have a dog so I couldn't tell him one. We have Booger but I didn't want to bore him to death.

I remembered the candy in my pocket. I reached in and pulled some out.

"You want some?" I said to Bob. "They all say the same thing."

I gave her a handful.

"My hands are clean," I said.

Bob took them and read the first heart.

" 'Good friend,' " she read.

"What?" I said.

She showed me the heart.

I reached into my pocket and took out the rest of the hearts. They all said, "Love is always present" in teeny tiny print.

Bob kept reading her hearts. "This one says I'm cute and this one says I'm special and this one says I'm lovable and . . ."

"Whatever," I said. The bell rang and I sat down.

Mr. Bernstein said, "Class, I need a volunteer to make our valentine box for those of you who want to give valentines to your classmates."

I raised my hand, but he didn't even look my way.

"Okay," he said, "Sybil and Scott, why don't you make us one? I've got a huge cardboard box and lots of stuff to use. Maybe you could start during lunch hour and stay a little after school?"

Sybil smiled too big. Someone should tell her she looks extra stupid when she does that.

"Great," Mr. Bernstein said.

"Great," I whispered through very tight lips.

Sybil the creep and Scott worked on the box during the lunch break and then stayed after school.

"It will be very cool," said Sybil.

"She thinks she is so darn hot," I said to Bob as we walked to the bus.

"Liz," she said, "you've got something hanging out of your hair."

I jumped around waving my arms because I thought she meant a spider. "Get it out! Get it out!" I screamed.

Everyone was looking at me.

"Hold still," said Bob. She looked closely at my hair.

"Uh-oh," she said.

"What do you mean uh-oh? Is it all falling out? Is it a scab?"

"No," she said quietly, "but it is kind of like . . . gum."

I couldn't believe it. I had gum stuck in my hair. How could that have happened? I could only think of one way. Someone put it there and I had an idea of who that someone was.

"Sybil," I hissed.

I had to ride all the way home with gum in my hair. I didn't want to say a word to anyone but I did.

"Stare at this a while," I said, flipping my gummy hair at the creepy boy behind me.

I stomped off the bus and stomped to my house and then I stomped to the kitchen and smeared peanut butter on my hair.

"Feel better now?" my dad said. He had decided to work at home that day.

"I have gum in my hair," I grunted.

"How . . ."

"Don't ask," I said. "Someone really hates me."

"I wasn't asking how you got it in there. I was impressed you knew how to get it out," he said cheerfully.

"It's happened before," I snapped, and went to the bathroom to wash my hair.

Someone was using water in the house so I could never get the shower the right temperature. Every time I got it right they'd turn on another faucet and I'd either scald or freeze myself.

"I can't believe it," I complained. "They won't even let me wash my hair in peace. Sybil is probably doing that, too."

I tried to think of things I could do to Sybil but

I was too mad to even be the least bit creative. The only thing I could think of was to yell at her. By the time I got out of the shower I was hopping mad. I even tried hopping to see if it would make me feel better but it only made my dad yell at me to stop.

I decided I was going to call her up. I went straight to the phone. Then I realized I didn't know her number, and on top of that I realized I didn't know her last name. I also didn't know her dad's or her mom's name.

"She did it to me again!" I screamed.

"Who?" said Booger.

"None of your business," I sneered.

Well, guess what? I got to do the dishes for being nasty at dinner. I also wasn't allowed to watch TV for calling Booger disgusting. Maybe we should go back to the fining system.

Look what Sybil did, I thought. *She got me mad so I'd be in trouble. She is such a creep.*

I went to bed mad. I woke up mad. I went to school mad. I walked into my classroom mad.

I was even madder when I saw the valentine box. It was huge all right. Ten times the size of any normal valentine box and it was absolutely beautiful. It was a miniature post office. I could've puked.

It wasn't fair. Mr. Bernstein must have helped them a ton. Why couldn't it have been slightly ugly? No, it had to have all kinds of three-dimensional-looking hearts on it and cupids and the colors all matched and everything. There were no scissor marks or pencil marks. Everything was perfect.

"Wow," said Monica.

"Wow," said Bob.

"Wow," said everyone who came into the room except me.

"It's okay," I said.

13

I was too busy concentrating on my anger so I didn't even notice that the crack was back, bigger than ever. I finally noticed when I saw the green ooze pouring into the room. It wrapped itself gently around the base of the perfectly stupid Valentine's Day post office. I looked around to see if anyone saw it.

Mr. Bernstein was overreacting about the box. Sybil was too busy acting like she was top loser in the Miss America pageant, which my mother won't let me watch because it is degrading.

Monica, who is part of the Sybil fan club, was saying, "Mr. Bernstein, we should take a picture of the box with Sybil and Scott beside it."

I could've spit venom out my mouth, nose, and ears. We have a class camera. We take pictures so we can photocopy them and make a year-end annual so everyone can sign it. I hardly thought this was something important enough to put in the annual.

"Good idea," said Mr. Bernstein. He was busy loading film into the camera.

I tried to get his attention to notice the crack.

"Mr. Bernstein . . . Mr. Bernstein . . . Hello? . . . Hello Mr. Bernstein? . . . Earth to Mr. Bernstein."

"In a minute," said Mr. Bernstein.

The foggy green ooze was getting thicker. I could barely see the stupid box or the stupid Sybil, which was a good thing.

"What's with the green fog?" I said to Bob who was right next to me.

"It's sunny outside," she said, looking puzzled.

"No," I said, "in here, the fog in here."

She didn't say anything.

"I'm not nuts," I said flatly. "You don't see the fog?"

"No," said Bob. "Are you okay?"

"Do you see that huge crack in the corner?" I don't know why I asked because I could no longer see it through the foggy ooze.

"You better go to the nurse," said Bob.

"I'm fine," I asserted.

At this point, I could barely see anything. However, I could hear Sybil irritatingly screaming that Mr. Bernstein had to wait a minute while she got her brush out of her backpack. Then I had a brilliant idea. Okay, I admit it was a totally stupid idea but at the time it seemed great. I thought, Wouldn't it be hysterical if I moved over there and jumped into the picture?

I walked toward the front of the class feeling my way and bumping into desks. I kept telling myself that the ooze was nothing and that I probably just needed glasses. I bumped into Megan and I stepped on Erin's toes who had to make a big deal out of it and yelled, "Ouch!"

"Sorry," I said, and instantly there looked like there was a break in the fog. "Well, thank goodness," I said, and the break got bigger.

Then I could see the box. The swirling foggy ooze now encompassed the whole room but was moving slightly away from the box. Sybil was standing guard two inches from her creation brushing her hair, madly trying to make it look good, which just wasn't going to happen. The ooze looked like it was waiting to attack the box and her. Sybil had made Scott stand right next to her.

Mr. Bernstein was saying, "Get ready. Say cheese. Say chocolate. Say something."

Scott said, "Cheese," and of course Sybil said, "Chocolate and lots of it."

"One, two, three," said Mr. Bernstein.

On three I ever so lightly shoved myself close to Scott's side and accidentally made him move an inch closer to Sybil. I didn't think it would kill him. Okay, how was I to know she was a complete klutz and couldn't stand on her own two feet? He barely brushed against her. Well, maybe I pushed myself a little harder than I needed to, but that still doesn't mean she shouldn't have kept her balance. I thought she took ballet and gymnastics.

Anyway, as the flash went off, Sybil fell sideways into her lovely little post office. One would think she would just move it a little or maybe whack it hard enough so it was completely wrecked. Then someone, who really knew how to make one, would have to decorate the new one. No, she had to fall smack dab inside the valentine box.

Now when I mean inside the box, I mean inside. They had drawn this slot where they were going to have us drop our valentines in but they hadn't cut it open yet. Well, get this. The drawing of the slot opened up like a huge black mouth of a cave and pulled her in. It swallowed her whole with this amazing sucking noise. Instinctively, Scott grabbed her arm and was pulled in with her. I was about to grab Scott but then Mr. Bernstein came charging over, pushing everything aside including me.

"What the hey?!" he yelled.

He grabbed Scott's legs, which were all that was left hanging out of the box. Suddenly something jerked, like a shark was eating them in big chunks, and Mr. Bernstein was gobbled up by the box, too. I stood there totally amazed. Instantly the ooze started retreating into the crack like a huge vacuum cleaner was sucking it up. The opening of the valentine box was closing. I had to think fast. I knew that when it closed they were going to be gone. I had to try to save them. Like an Olympic diver on a diving board, I took three steps, drew my knee up to get a little spring, and then performed a perfect swan dive straight into the remaining opening of the valentine box.

14

I was falling down but I just as well could have been falling forward. When you don't know which way is up or down it all looks the same so it's a little hard to tell. I felt like I was going down. Then I landed with a heavy "poof" sound flat on my back.

I must have had my eyes closed because when I opened them I was in a totally different place and yes, I was a little bit scared. I had fallen onto one of those inflated mattresses that they have at carnivals for kids to jump on. I never go on those things because you have to take your shoes off. I'll take my shoes off but have you seen some of the socks that walk around in there? How do you feel about terminal athlete's foot? No thank you, so I was glad I had my shoes on.

Now here's a strange thing. I was lying on this plastic jumping thing, a huge inflated mattress, and looking up at a roof. It was a tent roof and I couldn't see a hole where I came through. There was no slit, no tear, no flap, nothing. There was no opening and there was no evidence that I fell through the roof.

"Don't think about it," I told myself, trying not to totally scare myself.

I took a quick look around me. The mattress was red and the roof was yellow. The sides were a mixture of red and yellow screen material. I could hear the hum of the machine that was blowing air into the mattress.

I bounced over to the door that was zipped shut. I unzipped it. It reminded me of camping and being in a tent. Our tent, however, was never this comfortable.

I stepped out into a full carnival. There were rides and games and food stands. There was everything a carnival should have except people. It was very quiet for a carnival.

"Hello?" I ventured.

There was no response and I got a little spooked. I felt like I was being watched. There were so many places to hide. Someone could be out there, anywhere.

"Mr. Bernstein? Scott?" I called out. There was no answer, just the swinging of one of the seats on the Ferris wheel.

Suddenly I realized it was summer and how pleasant that felt. It was warm with just a light breeze blowing the flags on top of all the booths and the rides. The carnival had grassy areas around the rides and little paths leading you to each place. I could smell corn dogs and cotton candy and candy apples. None of the rides around me were running. I seemed to be in the preschool area with the little rides.

I wondered where all the people were. I was getting a funny feeling. I've never felt that safe at carnivals. There were too many stories about bad things happening and people getting ripped off. I was so weirded out that I called out, "Anyone there?"

Then I heard something.

"Lizzie? Is that you?" yelled Scott.

"Scott, where are you?" I yelled back.

"Up here!" he called out.

I looked over toward where his voice was coming from and sure enough he was on one of the seats of the Ferris wheel, clear at the top. I ran over.

"How in the world did you get up there?" I hollered to him.

"I don't know," said Scott. "I was asleep and I woke up here . . . I guess. When did we go to the carnival?"

"Can you see anyone?" I asked.

Scott looked all around. "No," he said, "but it's a huge carnival."

"Well how are you going to get down?" I asked.

"You'll have to start the machine," he said.

"Ya, right," I said. "I don't know how."

"Look around for a button," he suggested.

Well I was busy looking around for a button and I hadn't pressed anything, yet the Ferris wheel started on its own.

"Oh no," I screamed over the sound of the engine. "What have I done?"

I was thinking about how I was going to stop it. I yelled at Scott to get ready to jump out when he got close to the ground. But just as his seat got to the bottom, the Ferris wheel stopped.

"Thanks," said Scott to me.

"I didn't do anything," I said.

"Then who did?" asked Scott.

"Okay, you're now freaking me out," I told Scott. "We are in a haunted carnival and if there is one thing I hate, it is haunted carnivals."

"Have you ever been in a haunted carnival?" asked Scott.

I paused and thought. "No," I answered, "but I still hate them."

"Where's Sybil?" said Scott.

"Mr. Bernstein must be here, too," I said.

"How did we get here?" Scott said with this incredibly confused look. "The last thing I remember was getting my picture taken and then Sybil fell into the valentine post office."

"That is about what happened," I explained, "but you also followed Sybil, which wasn't a very smart thing to do if you ask me. Then Mr. Bernstein followed you and I dove in to save you all which probably wasn't a very smart thing to do either."

"Really?" said Scott in total disbelief.

"I'm not lying," I said. "I promise."

"Where are Sybil and Mr. Bernstein?" asked Scott.

"That's a good question. They are probably here somewhere."

"Help me!" we heard a girl scream. "Make it stop!"

We ran from the Ferris wheel past the kiddie rides through the carnival. We could see up ahead that there were bumper cars and they were running. When I say running, I mean really running. They were doing the Indy 500 and some girl was being whipped around the rink so fast that for certain she'd have to move into a chiropractor's office.

"Let it be Sybil, please," I said under my breath and I knew I shouldn't have been thinking it because it was so mean.

"Sybil?" Scott yelled.

"Help!" she screamed back.

Suddenly like when I was looking for a button to start the Ferris wheel, the bumper cars stopped on their own. I then had the shock, I mean the drop dead shock of my life. Sybil wasn't really Sybil. She was me!

My mind was racing. I mean it. I was looking at the girl in the car and it was me. I looked down at myself and then looked at her and I swear to you she was me. There were two of me.

"Sybil, are you okay?" asked Scott as he helped her out of the car.

The other me said, "Ya, I think so, but my neck is killing me."

"No wonder," said Scott sympathetically.

Then the other me looked at me. "Lizzie, are you okay?"

"Am I okay? Who are you?" I demanded.

"I'm Sybil," the other me said. "Are you nuts?"

"Maybe," I said. "Is that Sybil?" I asked Scott.

"Ya," said Scott.

"Who am I?" I asked him.

"Lizzie," he said.

"We aren't the same?" I said.

"I repeat, are you nuts?" said the person that was me but was Sybil.

"I have a headache," I said.

"How did we get here?" asked Sybil. "Where are we? What happened?"

Scott tried to explain. "Well, we're in a carnival and I don't know what we're doing here or how we got here but . . ."

"I remember something," said Sybil, "I remember, I remember . . . Lizzie, you pushed me into our gorgeous Valentine's Day box and wrecked it."

"How could I wreck it?" I said to the me that wasn't me.

"You did and now we're here and where are we?" she whined.

I hate whining. It is especially ugly coming from a Sybil that looks like me. Why do I have to be the person to handle everything?

"Oh, get over it," I said. "So you don't know where you are. You look good," and I started laughing till I thought I was going to wet my pants because she looked like me. What a joke. I quit because it reminded me I really had to find a restroom.

Well, the Sybil who looked like me seemed calmer.

"Okay," she said, "what do we do?"

Scott looked at me like I was supposed to come up with something.

"Well," I said, "we stick together and I suppose we should find a phone or something or go to the main gate."

We started walking.

"Let's hold hands," said Sybil. "It makes me feel safer."

"I don't think so," I said, "but you guys can if you want."

"No, that's okay, if you don't want to," said my twin and then like changing the entire subject she said, "I'm starving. Can we get a corn dog?"

"Why not?" said Scott. "Who would know?"

"Are you insane? Don't you think we should

find Mr. Bernstein and get out of here?" I muttered.

"It will only take a minute," said Sybil.

"Whatever," I said, totally dazed. It is kind of a shock to see yourself acting like Sybil. It's really kind of sickening.

We went over to a corn dog stand. Sybil let loose a little Sybil shriek. She tries to make screaming sound cute. It isn't. She was looking in a mirror.

Finally, I thought, *she'll see what has happened. She'll see that she looks like me.*

"Look at my hair," she demanded. "Doesn't someone have a comb? I can't run around like this?"

"You look fine," said Scott. "Here, have a corn dog." He reached across the counter and grabbed two under the heating lamp. "Anything else?" he said to the Sybil that looked like me. He didn't offer me anything.

"No, I'm fine," I said. "Thanks for not asking."

"Can you get me a soda?" said Sybil in her whiny little voice.

I took a quick look in the mirror and there I was. It was me. I hadn't changed. Why did Sybil look like me?

"Look," squealed Sybil, "fun house mirrors. I think they are so hysterical. Let's go see ourselves."

"I've seen quite enough fun," I said. "We have to

find Mr. Bernstein and a way back to our class."

"Ya, whatever," said Sybil as she ran over to the mirrors.

Scott and I followed her, walking.

"Look," she said, laughing and pointing to a mirror, "I'm fat."

I looked in the mirror and she wasn't fat but she was Sybil. I mean this time she was truly Sybil. She didn't look like me.

I looked at the real her or maybe it was the un-real Sybil. She still looked like me. Then I looked in the mirror at myself. I looked fat and like myself.

"Look," chirped Sybil, "let's go play some carnival games. Maybe we'll win something."

"You look," I said. "Do you not get that we are probably in danger here? We don't know where we are and we got here through your ugly Valentine's Day post office."

"Oh, come on," said Sybil, "be a sport. Scott? Are you coming?"

"Scott," I said, "we have to find Mr. Bernstein and get out of here."

"Okay," he said, "we will, just a second."

He went running off after my twin sister Sybil.

15

I spotted a restroom sign and went over to it. I had been waiting forever and I couldn't wait any longer. I went in. I was afraid that someone would be in there or would trap me or something but I wasn't going to tell Scott or Sybil because I didn't want them to make fun of me.

I checked all the stalls. No one was there. I locked the door and hurried. Then I was standing at the sink washing my hands and I looked up into the mirror. Scream time!

There was that man — Ralph — in the mirror, standing behind me. I whipped around to yell at him for being in the ladies' restroom and for scaring me to death. The only thing was, he wasn't there. I looked back in the mirror.

"What?" I groaned.

He was there in the mirror waving at me. I turned around again. He wasn't behind me. I looked in the mirror. There he was. I was getting dizzy. I wanted out of there.

"Wait," said Ralph.

"No!" I screamed at him.

"I'm sorry for frightening you but a gentleman usually doesn't enter a women's restroom."

"Oh, really," I said, "then why are you here?"

"Who says I'm here?" said Ralph with a smirk on his face.

"And who said I'm staying here to listen to you?" I said back at him.

"I do like you, Lizzie," he said.

"Then don't call me Lizzie," I said, not meaning to sound as cranky as I did.

"Okay, Liz, time for some straight talk," he said seriously.

"I'm waiting," I said with my arms crossed.

"You need to get out of the carnival before dark," he cautioned.

"Gladly," I agreed. "How?"

"Two things," he said, "and you must remember."

"I try to remember," I pouted. "I write myself notes."

He nodded. "I know. Remember this. You don't have to look for love. Love is always present. You only have to remove your blocks to seeing love's presence."

"What are the blocks? How is that supposed to help us?" I asked.

He laughed but I was serious.

"Who does Sybil look like?" he asked me.

"Right now?" I asked him back.

"Yes," he said.

"Well if you haven't noticed, she looks like me," I stated.

"Indeed," laughed Ralph.

"Did you do that?" I demanded.

"You're doing it."

"That is totally insane," I said.

"Do you remember your basement?" said Ralph.

"We're not going to do basements again are we?" Then something dawned on me. "You're the one that told me on the loudspeaker to go to the basement."

"You are brilliant! I knew you could do it," he exclaimed.

"What? What? What did I do?" I said, almost excited just because he was.

"I'll give you a huge clue," he said. "Sybil is your basement."

"Is this a joke?" I responded. "Because if it is a joke, it isn't funny."

"Your image of Sybil is only a reflection of something you don't want to face inside you. Look inside and you'll see her differently. I promise. I have to go now," he said.

"Wait!" I said. "You have to tell me how to get us out of here. What happens when it gets dark?"

"The way out is always to go inward. Love is at the center of everything."

"At least draw me a map," I pleaded.

He was fading in the mirror. "Remember love is at the center of everything . . . like the heart. Find your heart."

16

I stomped right out of that restroom, turning my back on that stupid Ralph. I was stomping and not thinking about anything except being mad at Ralph. What were we supposed to do? Now we had to worry about it getting dark. I could only imagine what happened to the carnival at night.

I was thinking about Ralph and the dark carnival so I didn't notice that I had stomped right through an open door and down a complete flight of stairs. Now I was smack dab in the middle of a basement parking garage without any cars. In one parking space close to some stairs was a video arcade game.

"Give me a break!" I said, raising my voice to heavy metal level. "It isn't funny."

I started to go back up the stairs when suddenly the game started up. It freaked me out so much I bolted up the stairs two at a time without taking a breath. The door was closed and it was locked. I pulled and rattled it and beat on it with my fists. I kicked it till my toes hurt. Then I cried. I hate, I mean I *hate* being locked in the basement.

"This isn't fair," I wailed.

Meanwhile, the game was playing a cheerful little computerized fakey tune.

"Stop it!" I yelled down to it.

It got louder. I stopped crying because I realized that if it was a parking garage it had to have another way out. I completely grossed myself out by wiping my nose on my sleeve but I didn't have anything else to wipe it on. I know, I'm as bad as Booger. I went back down the stairs and my plan was to go cautiously around the arcade game and find another exit.

I got close enough to peek at it. I was prepared for the worst and ready to run. I don't know what I expected. I guess I thought I'd see one of those stupid fighting games. I was afraid the characters would pop out of the screen and start fighting me. I didn't know. Anything could happen.

The music stopped and out of curiosity I moved closer to see the screen. On it was a pretty good picture of me and the name of the game, *Lizzie's Basement.* I moved even closer.

"Very funny," I said, and I wasn't laughing.

"Press start," prompted the screen.

The start button was blinking. I walked over and hesitantly pressed it.

Then on the screen was a continual flow of balloons with none other than Sybil's picture on them. On the end of the strings attached to each balloon was a card with some words on it. A cartoon character that I assume was supposed to be me was in a little helicopter. I had some kind of laser or something and I was supposed to shoot the balloons that were carrying cards that listed things about Sybil I didn't like. There was no end to the balloons so I had lots to choose from. I started blasting away.

"Oh . . . selfish, yes she is. Snooty, uh-huh. Take that. Nasty to people? Yes indeedy." The balloons kept coming and I probably could have hit them all if I had had more time. It isn't like I could run out of things to dislike about Sybil. However, the time was up and the screen went blank for a second.

Then there was this tree on the screen with some red fruit. I guess they were supposed to be apples. They had labels on them like *"Talented,"* and *"Cute."*

"What dumb graphics," I said.

Then a blue-and-green dragon with blinking green eyes appeared under the tree. A scroll unrolled on the screen and told me I had to move the dragon. Then I had to make it eat all the things I was jealous of about Sybil that were falling from the tree. It counted down from 10, 9, 8, 7, 6, 5, 4, 3, 2 . . . 1.

"Fine," I screamed at the machine.

I moved the dragon around, making him jump, fly, and even do flips. I opened its mouth catching *popular*, *cute*, *artistic*, *boys like her*, and *athletic* before the time was up. I thought that was pretty good for my first time and I waited to see what my score was going to be.

"Good," was all the screen said although the dragon got on his hind legs and did a dance like he'd scored a touchdown.

"Big deal," I scoffed.

Next the screen said, "Answer the following questions *yes* or *no* using the top green button for *yes* and the bottom blue button for *no*. This is a speed test. Answer the questions as rapidly as you can without stopping. Failure to answer correctly three times will result in termination of the game. You lose."

"Terrific," I said. "So I lose. So what?"

The first question was, "Have you ever been selfish?"

How can you answer that *yes* or *no*. *Sometimes* would be a good answer. *Maybe* would be another excellent answer. I needed it to be a multiple-choice question. I decided to press *no*.

Bells, beeps, quacks, and buzzers went off and the screen looked like there had been an explosion. "Wrong Answer" flashed on the screen. "Two more tries allowed."

"Fine, you stupid game," I said, and I hit the

yes button instead. "If you think I'm going to argue with a game, you're nuttier than I am." The noise stopped.

The next question was, "Have you ever been snooty to anyone?"

Not intentionally is the real answer so I pressed *no*.

This time as the screen turned into a giant fireball it sounded like a fire truck was coming out of the machine. I had to cover my ears to keep from going deaf. On the screen was "Wrong Answer and you only have one more chance before termination!"

"This is so retarded and unfair," I said. "Fine the answer is *yes*. I've been snooty. Are you happy?"

Then it asked me if I'd ever been nasty to anyone. I gave up and pressed the green button just to get it over with.

A huge red heart appeared in the center of the screen. Little white birds flew around and over it.

"Have you ever been popular? Cute? Athletic? Artistic? Have boys ever liked you?"

"Now this is more like it," I said as I pressed *yes*, *yes*, *yes*, *yes*, and *yes*.

"Game Over," said the screen. "You're free to go."

"That is it?" I spit out. "I don't get it."

I turned around and marched back up the stairs.

17

"Where have you been?" Scott asked me as I stepped out into the light.

I did notice that it was fading light. The sun was very low on the horizon.

"Oh," I said, "it's a long story. I was stuck in the parking garage playing a video game."

He looked at me, puzzled. "Shouldn't we be trying to get home or find out where we are?"

"Yes," I said. "I'm all for it. We have to find Mr. Bernstein first. Where's Sybil?"

"That is why I was looking for you. She went toward the games but then I lost her." He pointed back toward the Ferris wheel.

"We could leave her here if she's going to run off like that," I suggested.

"I thought I saw Mr. Bernstein and I yelled at him and he turned around," said Scott, ignoring my great recommendation. "I couldn't tell for sure if it was him. I'm sure he saw me but he just kept walking away. When I turned around Sybil wasn't there."

"Weird," I said. "I bet it wasn't him. It was probably Ralph."

"Who's Ralph?" Scott asked.

"Oh," I sighed, "just someone I know. It's hard to explain but he told me we have to get out of here."

"I guess we'd better go find Sybil," he said.

"I guess," I repeated. "Which way did she go again?" I still felt like leaving her.

We walked toward the Ferris wheel calling for her like a lost dog.

"Here Sybil!" I hollered. "C'mon Sybil. Where are you? Come out, come out wherever you are."

Then we went beyond the Ferris wheel into the carnival games. Right at the beginning of the row of game booths was an automatic fortune-telling machine. It was the kind that looks like a robot magician in a phone booth. Now there were two strange things about this fortune-teller.

Number one was that Sybil was the fortune-teller. Get this. She was in the sealed glass booth. I kid you not. She is so stupid. Number two was she no longer looked like me, she looked like her old ugly self.

We tapped on the window.

"Sybil," I demanded, "get out of there. What are you doing in there? You are so in trouble and that turban looks stupid. You don't fool anyone with that fakey painted-on mustache either."

She nodded her head like a mechanical doll. She looked especially weird, like she was in a trance.

"Maybe it isn't her," said Scott, trying to inspect her closely through the glass. "I don't think she's breathing."

"It's her all right," I said. "Let me tell you. I'd know Sybil anywhere and look at those flabby nostrils. She's breathing. She thinks she's pulling a funny one but the joke is on her because I don't think she's funny."

We went around to the back side of the machine. There was no door we could find. We searched the entire booth.

"She got in through the top," I guessed.

"Well . . ." stammered Scott, "what do you suggest?"

"Well," I said, "we can stay here and look at her, which is probably what she wants, or we can leave her and she'll probably come running. I vote for ditching her."

Right then a fortune came out of the tray in the front of the booth.

"Help me," it said.

We both slightly freaked out.

I yelled right up to the glass, "Can you breathe?"

Sybil didn't move.

"Boost me to the roof," I said.

Scott made a foothold with his hands and I

stepped on it. I then reached as high as I could, grabbing the top of the booth. Scott put his hands under my feet and pushed. That would've been fine except he pushed too hard and I went flopping on top of the roof like a fish landing in a boat. My torso was hanging headfirst over the opposite edge and my toes were gripping the other side.

"Are you trying to kill me?!" I screamed as I tried to pull myself up with my hands, but all I was doing was making the booth tip.

"Oh, no," I yelled. "Scott, help," but it was too late. The booth was going over and I was heading straight for the grass.

The next thing I knew, Scott and Sybil in that ridiculous turban and mustache were kneeling over me and saying, "Are you all right?"

"What?" I managed to say.

"Is anything broken?" said Scott.

"I hope not," I answered while trying to move myself.

"Maybe you shouldn't move," said Sybil. "You should wait for an ambulance."

"Like one is on the way," I said abruptly. "I'm fine." I sat up and brushed my arms off. "The grass broke my fall."

"You were amazing," said Scott, all excited. "You did a tuck and roll. You looked like a martial arts master or something. It was cool."

"Oh, really?" I smiled and was suddenly in a much better mood. "I did that?"

I was now standing up.

"And," said Sybil, "you saved my life," and she hugged me with her mustache and everything.

Okay, I let her hug me. It was no time to be mean. She was obviously shaken up and she did have a mustache. I was not completely sure that I could handle it but for an instant I didn't dislike her. I don't want to admit it but it felt good.

"What were you doing in there?" I asked. "Were you trying to fool us?"

"I don't know what happened," she told us, starting to cry. "I couldn't find you guys and I saw the fortune-teller. I started feeling funny. Then a fortune came out and it said to stand closer to the glass. I did and then everything went black. The next thing I knew I was inside the booth. I was stuck in there. I couldn't move except to nod my head up and down. I've never felt so afraid in my life."

"I think we'd better get out of here," said Scott, checking around us.

"Look," I said, seeing something out of the corner of my eye. "There goes Mr. Bernstein."

"Mr. Bernstein," Scott and I yelled. Sybil was too busy crying.

"Do you have a tissue?" she asked me.

"No," I said. "Use your sleeve and don't smear your mustache."

18

We hadn't had time to notice before because Sybil had to go be a fortune-teller, but it had moved quickly from sunset to dark. I remembered what Ralph had said. The lights of the carnival were more visible and the whole place was changing. I was positive that things had moved. They didn't seem in the same place. The Ferris wheel used to be right over there behind us. It wasn't there. I couldn't even get my bearings for the part of the carnival we had explored.

It wasn't as warm out either. The breezes had turned to wind and I wished I had a sweatshirt. Then I thought I heard some high-pitched shrieks coming from one of the throw-up rides. You know, the ones guaranteed to make you hurl. I knew there was no one really there.

I was going to ignore it but Sybil said, "What was that?"

"Probably nothing," I lied. "Do you believe in ghosts?" I asked Scott.

"C'mon," said Scott, "let's find the exit to this place."

"Well," said Sybil, "if Lizzie wants to."

I couldn't believe this was the same Sybil. Why would she care what I wanted to do?

"No, I have an idea," I said. "When I was in the restroom, Ralph said something about the center . . . I think he was telling us to keep going to the center."

"Where is that?" snapped Scott.

"Don't get mad at me," I said. "I'm just repeating what I was told."

"How do we know where the center is?" asked Sybil.

"How will we get out from the center?" said Scott. "That doesn't make sense. We should head for the exit."

Then out of the blue Sybil said, "I think we should try Liz's way first."

"I think it is the only way out," I stated.

Scott thought about it a minute. It was two against one. "Well," he said, "I guess it doesn't matter, because we don't know which way goes to the center or not. I think we should probably just get moving."

Suddenly, the rides were all starting up. Carnival music was everywhere.

"Whatever we do we should hurry because I have a bad feeling about this place at night. Like I don't think we should be here." Scott thought he needed to remind us.

Right then the carousel started and there is no way to describe it except the horses looked wild and fierce and their eyes were looking at us. They were almost alive.

"Well . . ." I shot back, "it is time to move."

We took off as fast as we could through the carnival. Well, some of us took off. Sybil was standing frozen to the ground in front of the carousel.

"What's wrong?" I said.

"I'm scared." She started crying.

"Well, so am I," I said, "but you can't let that stop you."

"But we don't know where we're going," said Sybil.

"It's never stopped me before," I said, feeling more brave.

"Me neither," said Scott.

"Can we hold hands?" asked Sybil.

Yes, we held hands with Scott in the middle. We ran like crazy in between rides and booths and along paths that led nowhere but back where we started. We were panting.

"We're getting nowhere," said Scott.

"We have to find the center," I reminded him.

"But we don't know where it is or what it is!" shouted Scott.

We heard another scream and the sound of a man yelling something in a strange language. It wasn't friendly sounding at all.

"What does a center look like?" asked Sybil.

I was stumped, scared, and cold. I stuck my hands in my pockets to get them warm. I felt something. It was one of the candy hearts from breakfast.

"How could I have missed it?" I said. "I am so stupid. The heart is at the center."

"Then that must be the center," Scott yelled, pointing to a giant pink neon-lit heart to our left. "Was that there before?"

"Who cares?" I said with more confidence than I had two minutes earlier. "The heart is the center."

"There's the guy I saw," shouted Scott.

We started moving toward him. We heard dogs or maybe even wolves over the sounds of the carnival behind us. I had a sideache but believe me I kept running.

We saw the man again. He was faster than we were. I didn't think we could catch up to him and I wasn't sure we even wanted to. He ran where the giant heart was. We reached him just as he jumped on the ride. It looked like a small rowboat and it was floating into a dark opening in the giant heart.

"It's the Tunnel of Love," I said, disgusted with myself for not thinking of it sooner.

"Let's go," said Scott, grabbing the side of one of the boats.

Without pausing to consider the insanity of it, I jumped into the little boat and Scott was right behind me.

"Jump!" we screamed at Sybil.

"I can't," said Sybil running and hopping on the edge of the canal, "I won't make it."

"Stop hopping and jump," I commanded her while reaching out my hand.

She grabbed my arm tight enough to break it and jumped on top of us, nearly tipping over the boat. It was just in time because we were entering the open mouth leading into a dark tunnel.

"I'm still scared," said Sybil.

"Really?" I said sarcastically.

"It's the Tunnel of Love," said Scott, trying to be cute. "What can happen to us?"

"I just wish I had a life jacket," I said.

"Why?" asked Sybil.

"Do you hear that noise?" I asked, hoping it was all in my imagination.

"What noise?" said Sybil. "I can't hear anything besides that roaring noise."

It was getting much louder. I mean much louder.

"I *mean* the roar," I said.

"What?" yelled Sybil. "I can't hear you."

"It sounds like white water," shouted Scott loudly trying to be heard.

"Ya," I screamed, "it sounds like . . . Niagara Falls. . . . Hang on!"

19

Here is all I can tell you about what happened because it is all I know. We heard the sound of a huge amount of rushing water. There was nothing to do but listen because we couldn't see anything. It was a total blackout in the tunnel. Then the boat went out from under us.

We were falling. I thought we were going to die. I nearly had a heart attack. We tried to hang on to each other but couldn't. Then suddenly it all stopped. I was sitting with my knees in my chest. I was totally squished into a tiny little space and very close to someone, actually two someones.

It was dark and my eyes were trying to adjust.

"Scott?" I hoped he was okay.

"Lizzie? Is that you?" he answered.

"Who do you think it is?"

"I don't know," said Scott, acting like he was in a total fog. "Why am I here?"

"Scott? Lizzie? What happened?" said Sybil, acting like a total airhead.

"Why am I in here?" repeated Scott.

"Where are we?" asked Sybil. "And why am I all wet?"

"We went over a waterfall or something," I said, as clearly and slowly as possible so that the two morons might understand.

"Huh?" said Scott, totally confused.

"You know," I said impatiently. "We were in the Tunnel of Love and now we're here."

I couldn't exactly see their eyes in the dark but I didn't have to to know they were looking at me like I was totally and inescapably nutso.

"Let me guess," I said. "You both remember nothing?"

"About what?" said Scott.

"The carnival, maybe?"

"A carnival?" said Sybil.

"Ya," I explained, "we fell into the Valentine's Day post office box and then we were at this carnival and we were trying to find Mr. Bernstein and we thought we saw him going into the Tunnel of Love at the center of the carnival and you have absolutely no idea what I'm talking about do you?"

"Maybe you could just tell us where we are now?" suggested Scott.

"I don't know, but it must be some kind of box," I said, feeling the floor and sides where I was crunched. "Sybil, could you move your elbow? It's poking me . . . thanks."

Then we could hear muffled voices around us. The question is whether they were friendly or not.

"Are we safe?" whispered Sybil.

"I guess there is only one way to find out," I said. "We have to break out and be ready for anything."

Scott liked that idea. Some boys like anything as long as it sounds risky.

"I think it's only cardboard," said Scott. "It feels like a cardboard box. We should be able to bust it open pretty easy."

"Okay," said Sybil.

"Okay," I agreed.

"On three then," said Scott.

"Wait," I interrupted. "What are we doing?"

"We'll just push our backs against it," said Scott. "One, two . . ."

He didn't get to three because when he reached "two" the top of the box opened and staring down at us was Mr. Bernstein.

"That is where you guys were hiding," he said cheerfully, like it was a game and he was having a good time. I was confused. He wasn't angry with us at all and he wasn't wet. "We couldn't find you anywhere," he laughed.

Sybil and Scott laughed along with him and I knew they didn't have a clue. Some people are so strange. The class crowded around the box to peek at us.

"Maybe we could have some help out?" I suggested.

"Absolutely," said Mr. Bernstein.

He grabbed my hand and helped me out.

"You're all wet," he observed. "How did that happen?"

I started to tell him, but by then Scott was out of the box and he interrupted me and said, "We don't know," which was hardly an answer.

"Actually we were looking for you," I started, "and . . ."

Sybil stood up and everyone flipped. They were laughing hysterically.

"What? What?" she kept repeating.

There was Sybil, soaking wet, with a turban and a mustache.

20

"Why won't you let me finish our story?" I whispered to Scott.

"Because it isn't true," he said.

"It is, too," I whispered louder.

"You're crazy," he said very loudly.

"Oh, really," I said quite calmly.

Sybil was still saying "What? What?" till you just wanted to slap her silly.

Mr. Bernstein was getting us things to wear out of the costume box while our clothes dried.

"Great," I said flatly when he handed me the clown suit, and Sybil the princess dress. Scott could only fit into an angel robe. So he got to be a Christmas angel but without a halo. He was a gray Christmas angel because that costume could've used a little bleach. It was still better than the clown suit.

We went down the hall to change our clothes in the restroom. Sybil took a look in the mirror and lost it.

"What happened to me? Look at me. I have a mustache. Why do I have a mustache?"

I don't know what I was thinking except she was close to crying. I put my arm around her. "It's okay," I said. "Just wash it off."

"Everyone was laughing at me," she said.

"Ignore them," I said and then I couldn't believe what popped out of my mouth. "They're just jealous."

We looked at each other in the mirror. We both started to say something to each other's reflection in the mirror. It's so weird to talk to someone that way. We stopped, laughed, and looked at each other for real.

"What?" I said.

"No, go ahead," said Sybil.

"I forget," I lied.

"I was going to say thanks, you're a true friend," said Sybil. "I feel like we're a lot alike."

"Really?" I said in disbelief.

"You know what? I've always wanted to be your friend but I didn't think you liked me," said Sybil, and I think she meant it.

Okay, so I lied again. Sue me. "Oh," I said, "I've always liked you. I thought you didn't like me."

"That is so sweet," said Sybil.

I thought, *But if you think I'm joining your fan club you're crazier than I am.*

"Well." I broke our great moment. "I have to

put the clown suit on and you get to be the beautiful princess."

She laughed and then she stopped and looked at me. She held out the princess dress and said, "Here, you be the princess. I'll be the clown."

I don't know. I wasn't used to this. Sybil being nice to me was something I'd have to get used to. I wasn't sure whether to trust her or not.

"Thanks," I said, "but I'll take the clown suit. You're more the princess type."

"Are your sure?" she offered.

"Ya, but thank you, really," I said, trying to sound sincere because I really meant it.

We got dressed and walked back to class. Sybil looked great. I looked like a clown who had wadded up his costume, put it in a box and let it get severely wrinkled.

"Are you sure you don't remember anything that happened?" I questioned Sybil.

"No." She looked puzzled. "Were we playing a game?"

"How'd you get the mustache?" I tried to get her to remember. "The fortune-teller?"

"All I remember — " started Sybil but then Scott came out of the boys' room.

"I look stupid," said Scott.

"No stupider than I look," I said. We both looked at Sybil, who didn't look stupid at all.

Scott said to me, "At least you're warm. I have on a dress."

"It's a dirty dress, too," I laughed.

He cracked up. "I keep trying to remember something but I guess I got abducted by aliens. I can't remember how we got wet or how we got in the box."

"I told you," I said.

"That doesn't make sense," he said.

"What does then?" I demanded.

"I don't know" is all he could say.

"Wait, wait, I remember something," said Sybil, stopping dead in her tracks and trying hard to concentrate. "Something is at the center. That's it! Something is both at the center but . . . I don't know what."

"It's love," I said softly as we entered the class.